Fir Tree Circus

Written by
Laura Appleton-Smith

Illustrated by
Keinyo White

Laura Appleton-Smith holds a degree in English from Middlebury College.
Laura is a primary school teacher who has combined her talents in creative writing with
her experience in early childhood education to create *Books to Remember*.
She lives in New Hampshire with her husband, Terry.

Keinyo White is a graduate of the Rhode Island School of Design with a B.F.A. in illustration.
He currently produces children's books and freelance illustrations
from his studio in Los Angeles.

A Book to Remember™
Published by Flyleaf Publishing

For orders or information, contact us at **(800) 449-7006**.
Please visit our website at **www.flyleafpublishing.com**

Eighth Edition 2/20
Library of Congress Catalog Card Number: 2012939859
ISBN-13: 978-1-60541-128-6
Printed and bound in the USA
243081021A28

Chapter 1

In a hidden spot in the forest stands a big fir tree.

This hidden spot is tranquil and still but for the stir of the wind as it swirls in the tree's branches.

The bottom branches of the fir tree hang in an emerald skirt that rests over the moss bed under the tree.

It is as if the branches have formed a fantastic hidden tent.

If a girl happened past this spot, she might stop
to sit on the moss and rest her back
on the firm trunk of the tree.

And if the wind did not lull her to curl up and have a nap, she just might witness what happens under the fir tree at dusk.

Chapter 2

The lightning bugs collect in the branches of the fir tree and cast their light onto the moss bed...

and birds lift up tendrils from plants
and use them to construct nets and swings.

Then the strong ants enter. They bring in rock after rock until they have enough rocks to construct a big circle in the dirt.

The forest animals gather to sit on logs and on the moss bed.

Chapter 3

Then there is a sudden "bang, bang, bang" of a drum. It is the mantis ringmaster. "Animals of the forest, the Fir Tree Circus has begun!"

A blur of squirrels bursts into the tent, jumping and twirling and spinning.

The biggest squirrels toss the littlest squirrels up into the tip-top of the tent.

The little squirrels spin as they drop
and land in soft web nets.

Every forest animal claps or honks or purrs
for the fantastic stunts, "More! More!"

For the next act, the bobcat enters.
The animals murmur because a vivid butterfly
is sitting on the bobcat's back.

When the butterfly swirls in circles,
the bobcat turns around in circles.

As the butterfly stops, the bobcat stops.

When the butterfly lifts her wing, the bobcat stands up.

"How can it be?" the animals murmur.

Chapter 4

Just then, a big gust of wind puffs.
The tendrils drop back onto the moss bed,
and the animals run back into the forest.

And under the light of dusk,
a girl who was lulled into a nap…

might wonder what had been happening
as she was sleeping…

when she spots a circle of rocks in the dirt.

Prerequisite Skills

Single consonants and short vowels
Final double consonants **ff**, **gg**, **ll**, **nn**, **ss**, **tt**, **zz**
Consonant /k/ **ck**
/ng/ **n[k]**
Consonant digraphs /ng/ **ng**, /th/ **th**, /hw/ **wh**
Schwa /ə/ **a, e, i, o, u**
Long /ē/ **ee, y**
r-Controlled /ûr/ **er**
/ô/ **al, all**
/ul/ **le**
/d/ or /t/ **–ed**

Target Letter-Sound Correspondence

r-Controlled /ûr/ sound spelled **ir**

birds	squirrels
fir	stir
firm	swirls
girl	twirling
skirt	

Story Puzzle Words

begun	circus
branches	enough
chapter	forest
circle	formed
circles	lightning

Target Letter-Sound Correspondence

r-Controlled /ûr/ sound spelled **ur**

blur	murmur
bursts	purrs
curl	turns

High-Frequency Puzzle Words

around	of
be	or
because	over
been	she
for	their
from	there
have	they
how	to
into	use
light	was
might	what
more	who

Decodable Words

1	bobcat's	gather	little	run	the
2	bottom	gust	littlest	sit	them
3	bring	had	logs	sitting	then
4	bugs	hang	lull	sleeping	this
a	but	happened	lulled	soft	tip-top
act	can	happening	mantis	spin	toss
after	cast	happens	moss	spinning	tranquil
an	claps	has	nap	spot	tree
and	collect	her	nets	spots	tree's
animal	construct	hidden	next	stands	trunk
animals	did	honks	not	still	under
ants	dirt	if	on	stop	until
as	drop	in	past	stops	up
at	drum	is	plants	strong	vivid
back	dusk	it	puffs	stunts	web
bang	emerald	jumping	rest	sudden	when
bed	enter	just	rests	swings	wind
big	enters	land	ringmaster	tendrils	wing
biggest	every	lift	rock	tent	witness
bobcat	fantastic	lifts	rocks	that	